Chime #5
Travelers

Advance praise for *The Strangers at the Manger*

"Through her gifted storytelling, Lisa Hendey truly makes the Holy Family come alive. This book will help you and your children see Mary, Joseph, and Jesus as real people who lived, worked, and prayed with simple and humble faith, not just figurines in your nativity set. In this world filled with consumerism, give your children the gift of understanding the true story of Christmas and the joy that comes with 'welcoming the stranger' by sharing with them *The Strangers at the Manger*."
—Michele Faehnle, coauthor, *Divine Mercy for Moms,*
Sharing the Lessons of St. Faustina

"Lisa Hendey invites us to enter into the Christmas story with her beloved twin heroes, Patrick and Katie, as they learn firsthand how to welcome the stranger, share from the heart, and rekindle the joy of Jesus's birth. Through this festive, charming, and imaginative Chime Travelers book, the true meaning of Christmas will shine brightly in the hearts of children and parents alike."
—Sarah Damm, mom of six and editorial and marketing director
for WINE: Women in the New Evangelization

"This latest adventure with Chime Travelers Patrick and Katie is rich with warmth and charm. Lisa Hendey gives us a story that manages not only to bring young imaginations to the realities of Christ's birth, but also brings Christmas to life in the midst of our present-day experiences. Highly recommended—for all ages!"
—Erin McCole Cupp, author, *Unclaimed*

"This is a fantastic book. It reminds me of the Ignatian spiritual exercises, but for kids! What a terrific way for children to engage in the faith and in the Bible more deeply!"
—Christine Johnson, Catholic mom and blogger at DomesticVocation.com

franciscan
media
Cincinnati, Ohio

The Strangers at the Manger

LISA M. HENDEY
ILLUSTRATED BY JENN BOWER

Note: The following is inspired by the Infancy Narratives in the Gospels according to Matthew and Luke but is a work of fiction.

Cover and book design by Mark Sullivan

All illustrations by Jenn Bower

LIBRARY OF CONGRESS CATALOGING-IN-PUBLICATION DATA

Names: Hendey, Lisa M., author. | Bower, Jenn, illustrator.

Title: The strangers at the manger / Lisa M. Hendey ; all illustrations by Jenn Bower.

Description: Cincinnati, Ohio : Servant, [2016] | Series: Chime travelers ; 5 | Summary: "Patrick and Katie Brady are introduced to an immigrant family who recently arrived at St. Anne's Parish. A tinkling bell transports the twins to first-century Bethlehem, where they meet the Holy Family—and come to understand what it is like to be a stranger at the manger"— Provided by publisher.

Identifiers: LCCN 2016022338 | ISBN 9781632531001 (trade paper : alk. paper)

Subjects: LCSH: Jesus Christ—Nativity—Juvenile fiction. | CYAC: Time travel—Fiction. | Christian life—Fiction. | Immigrants—Fiction. | Compassion—Fiction. | Twins—Fiction. | Brothers and sisters—Fiction. | Jesus Christ—Nativity—Fiction. | BISAC: JUVENILE FICTION / Readers / Chapter Books. | JUVENILE FICTION / Religious / Christian / Action & Adventure. | JUVENILE FICTION / Religious / Christian / Historical.

Classification: LCC PZ7.1.H463 St 2016 | DDC [Fic]—dc23

LC record available at https://lccn.loc.gov/2016022338

ISBN 978-1-63253-100-1

Published by Franciscan Media
28 W. Liberty St.
Cincinnati, OH 45202
www.FranciscanMedia.org

Printed in the United States of America.
Printed on acid-free paper.
19 20 21 22 23   7 6 5 4 3

▲ Chapter One ▲

Brrriiinnnggg...

"We're outta here!" Patrick shouted when the dismissal bell chimed at St. Anne's School. He turned to fist-bump Pedro as his twin, Katie, hugged her best friend, Lily.

"Don't worry," Lily said. "I'll call you every day of break. And we'll go to extra riding lessons. Christmas break's gonna be a blast!"

"Class," their teacher called over the noise, "I'll see you at the Family Mass on Christmas Eve! Have a great break."

"You, too, Coach!" Patrick grabbed his soccer ball and backpack.

"What are you doing during Christmas break, Mr. Birks?" Katie asked. Now that Katie's hair was cut short, the twins looked more alike than ever. Even though they sometimes teased each other, they were best buddies, especially since their Chime Travel missions had started and they'd discovered some amazing adventures at and around St. Anne's!

"Just taking it easy. I'll see my family, and, of course, beat your dad and Fr. Miguel at basketball a few times! How about you two?" Mr. Birks smiled. "Any special missions planned?"

The twins looked at each other, surprised by Mr. Birks's use of the word *mission*. It was the same word they used when talking with each other about their Chime Travel adventures into the lives of saints. Both laughed nervously.

"Just trying to keep Hoa Hong from climbing

the Christmas tree!" Katie said. Their little sister was suddenly into everything. It had been more than a year since she'd come all the way from Vietnam to be a part of the Brady family, and she was a perfect fit. Hoa Hong, whose Vietnamese name meant "Rose," had Patrick's speed and Katie's spunk.

As the rest of the kids headed toward the parking lot, the twins noticed Fr. Miguel and Sr. Margaret enter the room with a small group of people.

Katie and Patrick stayed behind to take a closer look at the strangers. A tall, thin man stood closest to Fr. Miguel. He had tired eyes and a tense frown. Next to him was a woman who looked like she might burst into tears at any moment. She held the smallest baby the twins had ever seen. Behind them, an old man with silver hair held the hand of a little boy who was hiding behind his legs.

The adults spoke quietly to one another. Katie and Patrick watched, intrigued by the visitors. The boy looked up at the twins with wide, dark eyes. In one hand, he clutched a battered stuffed animal. He stared at them, his coal-colored eyes never blinking.

"I don't think he's seen red hair before," Katie whispered.

"Where do you think they're from?" Patrick asked. He dropped his voice even lower. "And is that smell coming from them?"

Katie wrinkled her nose. "I have no idea. Maybe Fr. Miguel found them wandering around the school and he's trying to get them out of here."

Fr. Miguel smiled at the twins from across the room and then addressed Mr. Birks. "Coach, this is the Perez family. They arrived this morning. We're finding them a safe place to stay tonight."

"Welcome," Mr. Birks said a little too loudly as he shook Mr. Perez's hand.

"Talking louder won't help them understand," Patrick snickered to his sister.

Katie elbowed him. "Shh!"

"Let's go." He tugged on Katie's backpack strap. "Mom's waiting." Something about the Perez family made Patrick uncomfortable. Besides, he was eager to get Christmas break started. Whoever these strangers were, he had more important things on his mind.

▲ Chapter Two ▲

Early in the morning on the day before Christmas, the Brady van pulled into the St. Anne's parking lot. Patrick yawned next to Katie. Then he burped and Hoa Hong dissolved into giggles.

"Gross!" Katie shoved his arm.

"Gwoss!" Hoa Hong echoed, still giggling.

"C'mon kids," Mr. Brady sighed. "It's Christmas Eve. Could we call a truce for the day?"

"Right. It's Christmas Eve," Katie agreed.

"So, why are we here already?" Patrick asked impatiently.

"Mom explained it last night," Katie said. "Cleaning Team has to get the church ready for Family Mass tonight. Christmas Eve and Christmas are pretty much the busiest days of the whole year for St. Anne's. The church doesn't just decorate itself!"

"Exactly," Mrs. Brady nodded as she pulled Hoa Hong from her car seat. "When we committed to being on Cleaning Team, we agreed to this. Remember, Patrick?"

Patrick thought about Hoa Hong's baptism last year when his pet frog Francis had jumped into the font of holy water. The Bradys had signed up for Cleaning Team after that, so the kids could learn more about their church, but they never could have imagined the adventures ahead of them. It was because of Cleaning Team that the twins discovered the whole Chime Traveler thing!

Patrick and Katie had each experienced some amazing "missions," traveling in time to meet different saints. It was a huge secret that the twins had decided to keep to themselves. They had figured out that the Chime Travel happened when bells rang. They also knew that they could only get back home once they'd learned an important lesson.

The twins had talked for hours about the different places and times they had each visited. They'd even started a wish list of future missions they hoped to take. But they knew they couldn't actually make Chime Travel happen. They had to wait for whatever their next adventure would be, while daydreaming about what saints they might get to meet.

"I know we have to do it," Patrick sighed. "And I like being here, usually, but my friends are having a multiplayer tournament online today. I'm probably going to miss the whole thing!"

"Lily and I wanted to meet at Reinhard's stables to take Peerybingle and Belle for a ride," Katie said.

"I know, kids." Mom sounded tired. "I've got a to-do list a mile long, too. I don't know how I'll ever get it all done by tonight. But we made a commitment."

The whole family paused for a moment to genuflect before the large crucifix, then immediately fell back into their mental lists of things they'd rather be doing.

"Well, hello, lovely Brady family!" Mrs. Danks chirped in her Irish accent as they entered the nave. The head of the Cleaning Team was holding her clipboard with a list of jobs to be done. "Thank you for spending the morning with us!"

Behind her, Fr. Miguel held the vacuum cleaner. "Hey, team!" he said cheerfully. "Happy Christmas Eve! Are we ready to make this church sparkle?"

The twins thought it was funny how much their pastor loved cleaning the church.

"There's no way I'd miss today!" the priest said. "Setting up the nativity scene is one of my very favorite things about Christmas! What do you say, Patrick and Katie? Wanna help me arrange some donkeys, camels, and sheep?"

"Sure thing, Padre," Patrick said. "As long as we're here, we might as well do the best job on Mrs. Danks's clipboard!"

▲ Chapter Three ▲

As Katie and Patrick walked up to the space for the St. Anne's nativity scene, they spotted the little boy they'd met the day school let out for Christmas break. He was huddled inside the large wooden stable.

Patrick saw the boy's worried parents searching the pews on the other side of the church. He elbowed Katie softly. "I think he's hiding."

The boy pulled something from the back pocket of his jeans and start to place it in the manger.

"Hey," Patrick warned, "watch out! You're gonna break something!"

"He doesn't know what you're saying," Katie whispered. "What is that thing in his hands?"

"It's his toy," Patrick answered. "It looks like some kind of um, animal, I think…"

Katie reached for the child, trying to remove him from the nativity without scaring him. "Oh, no, no, no…," she whispered. "That thing doesn't belong in here."

The boy looked at her with dark eyes as he climbed out of the nativity and said one word.

"Burro."

It was soft, almost a whisper. Then he clutched the animal back to his chest, and tears welled up in his brown eyes.

"Burro?" Katie repeated. "You mean donkey? Well, you should go back to your mom and dad. We wouldn't want you to break anything here." She backed away from the little boy a few steps. "He smells like a stable," she whispered to Patrick.

"Hey, Padre," Patrick yelled to Fr. Miguel, who was now helping the Perez family search. "The kid's over here!"

Mr. Perez and Fr. Miguel rushed toward the stable. It was really just a bunch of fence posts that Mrs. Danks's husband had painted and nailed together. Fr. Miguel somehow managed to make it look awesome every year.

Patrick turned to the little boy and teased, "Now you're about to get busted!"

"Don't scare him, Patrick," Katie said. "He's probably already afraid enough, coming to a totally new place!"

"I'm just joking," Patrick said. "Besides, he kind of looks like a troublemaker."

"It takes one to know one!" Katie shot back.

Mr. Perez hurried to the nativity and reached for his son. Even though the twins couldn't understand Spanish, they could guess what was happening as the dad led his son down the aisle toward his mom and sister. He shook a finger, talking a mile a minute.

"That one's a handful!" Fr. Miguel smiled. "I think he'll fit in around here!"

"What happened to them, Father?" Katie asked. "Why are they here?"

"I can't go into the whole story, Katie," the pastor answered. "But they needed a safe place to stay for a while, and we have room at the parish center. So, we're happy to take them in, especially at Christmas."

"Not exactly a good time of year to drop in without an invitation…. It's pretty lucky that you were even able to find room for them," Patrick said.

Fr. Miguel nodded. He looked back at the family of strangers. Sr. Margaret was about to take them to Catholic Charities to find warm clothes.

The priest shook his head. "Well, I think we've got some work to do around here…"

Patrick was already lining up the large nativity scene figures. With one hand he grabbed a sheep, and, with the other, he reached for a camel. Katie cautiously picked up the figures of Mary and Joseph. "Be careful," she said to Patrick. "Those are breakable!"

Near the altar, Mr. Sarkisian was gathering the members of the St. Anne's bell choir for their last music practice. The choir members put on white gloves, and each pulled their silver bells out of cases.

"Let's turn to our opening hymn," the choir director said. Everyone shuffled pages. They held their bells up, waiting for their director's signal to begin playing.

"Patrick," Katie scolded her twin, "you can't put that camel so close to the manger! The sheep are OK, but the camel needs to go over there, by the ambo!" She pointed across the sanctuary to the wooden stand where the lectors stood to read during Mass.

"But the camel's totally awesome! No one will even see it over there," Patrick argued.

"Well, there are no camels in Bethlehem until Epiphany!" Katie said, placing a donkey into the spot where the camel had been standing. "Besides, the donkey needs to go there!"

"The donkey," said Patrick, "is totally boring."

"Boring?! The donkey's the one who..."

"Kids," said Fr. Miguel, trying to make peace, "I think you're missing the point here."

"Yeah, Patrick," Katie said, "let's just get this done. Stick that camel over there by the wise men!" She gestured to three statues, each holding a different fancy-looking present.

"Whatever..." Patrick snorted, bending toward the camel statue.

Mr. Sarkisian was talking to the bell choir. "Ready?" he asked, lifting his arms high to begin the music.

Katie heard the first bright bell ring out the opening notes of a familiar carol.

"O, Come…"

Patrick turned his head as the second bell player shook one of her silver, long-handled bells.

"All…"

As the fourth note chimed out "Ye…", both twins felt an intense rush of cold wind. The ground around them began to rumble.

And suddenly, everything became a blur.

▲ Chapter Four ▲

The first thing that Patrick heard when the ground stopped rumbling was an odd combination of sounds.

Clank, clank.

Heehaw!

As he lifted himself to a standing position, his head swiveled in every direction. Patrick knew immediately that he'd Chime Traveled.

"You're here, too?"

Patrick whipped around at the sound of the familiar voice. It was Katie!

"We did it! We Chime Traveled together!" she

laughed, running toward him.

"Yeah," Patrick said. "The chimes…was it the bell choir?"

"Must have been!" Katie agreed. "But where are we, and when are we?"

"Let's find out," Patrick said, walking in the direction of the distant bell he heard. "That bell sounds a little like Adhamh's bell."

"The sheep? With St. Patrick?" Katie asked.

"Yep!"

They took off running down the rocky path toward the sound of the clanking bell.

"It sounds like a cowbell," Katie said. "But that doesn't sound like any cow I've ever heard before!"

"It's no cow. Look!" Patrick pointed to an animal in the field just beyond the olive trees.

"A donkey!" Katie said.

"Yep!" Patrick agreed. "Looks like he's tied to that tree over there."

"Maybe we should go check him out," Katie suggested. "He might be a clue to this mission."

"Good idea," Patrick smiled. Then he said shyly, "Hey, Katie?"

"Yeah?" Katie was distracted, trying to figure out who they might be about to meet.

"It's pretty cool that we're both here," Patrick said. Then he punched her softly in the shoulder and ran toward the grey donkey. His sister laughed and followed him.

"Awww, hey there, little guy," Katie said as she reached out to pet the animal's black mane. Suddenly, the donkey let out the loudest heehaw yet!

The kids laughed and then turned, startled, when a voice called out from some nearby rocks.

"Goodness, Nicholas! Are you ready to get on the road even before breakfast?"

Patrick and Katie saw a man emerge from the rock cave and walk toward them. He wore a long, tan robe that looked like it was made of scratchy material. He had a brown belt tied around his waist and some brown fabric stretched across his shoulders like a cloak. His head was covered with a dark green scarf that flowed down his back and was tied into place with a bit of rope. He hummed as he walked toward them, his long hair and beard blowing in the morning breeze.

The twins stood behind Nicholas the donkey, waiting to see what would happen next.

A young woman's voice called out from the cave, "Joseph? Is it time to depart already? It's still so early."

"Nicholas seems to think so," the man answered as he walked up to the tree. "And, if we leave now, we will arrive tonight, before it is too late." Then he spotted the twins, and Nicholas began his loud donkey braying.

Heehaw!

Clank, clank.

"Well, who do we have here, Nicholas?" the man said kindly as he approached.

"I'm Katie."

At the very same instant, her twin called out, "I'm Patrick."

"Greetings, my friends," the man said, offering Nicholas a handful of grain. "How have you found your way here? Are you two headed to Bethlehem for the enrollment? You must come from very far away to be wearing such interesting clothing!"

Both twins looked at each other in their jeans and hoodies. Katie's favorite red boots were as bright as poppies against the dusty ground. Their green eyes twinkled.

"Joseph?" Katie asked, again petting Nicholas, who was finally quiet.

"Bethlehem?!" Patrick repeated, a huge smile spreading across his face.

Joseph looked at the twins with a question in his eyes. Then he turned toward the morning sun, almost fully risen behind the cave and smiled, nodding his head.

"Mary," he called, "I think we have found some traveling companions for the last day of our journey!"

▲ Chapter Five ▲

"Can you believe it?" Patrick whispered to Katie. "Mary, Joseph, and a donkey? On the way to ⬛⬛⬛⬛⬛?"

Then in one breath, both twins agreed, "Best Chime Travel mission ever!"

Joseph untied Nicholas from the tree and led him toward the cave. The sturdy grey donkey seemed happy for the chance to stretch his legs.

"How can we help you?" Patrick asked. He was anxious to find a way for them to stick around for a while.

Katie suggested, "Let's go find some firewood."

"That would be helpful, thank you," Joseph said, smiling.

They spent the next few minutes in a small grove of gnarled olive trees, collecting fallen limbs and making a plan. They returned to Joseph, their arms overflowing with branches and twigs.

"Joseph?" Patrick asked, "How much longer until we get to Bethlehem?"

"Well, we've been on the road for five days now," Joseph said. "Nicholas could travel much faster. He is a strong donkey! But we need to move more slowly to keep Mary comfortable. The baby will be here any day."

"Nicholas is the very best donkey," Mary said, walking up to the fire. Katie and Patrick stood in stunned silence. Could it really be her?

"Will you join us?" she asked them. "You are very young to be traveling alone."

"We'd love to," Patrick answered. He could tell what Katie was thinking—Mary was very young!

And not dressed in blue. And no glowing halo floating around her head! Joseph was younger than they'd expected, too. Not the grey-haired old man they'd seen in books and statues around St. Anne's. He seemed just a little older than Mr. Birks.

Katie thought about how much Mary looked like some of the girls at Mater Dei, the high school down the street from St. Anne's. Mary wore a light-colored robe that was dusty from traveling. A scarf covered the back of her long brown hair. Her belly was enormous! But her smile was warm, and light shone from her eyes, even in the middle of a challenging journey.

"Shall we give thanks to God before enjoying our breakfast?" Mary asked. "You will join us? We would love to have you journey with us."

Katie saw the small loaf of bread that Joseph held and the few figs on the ground near the fire and thought that there was barely any breakfast for Mary and Joseph to eat. But Joseph insisted there was plenty to share. So the twins sat on the ground and ate their tiny portions.

"How did you get here?" Katie asked Mary.

"It was a normal day, like any other," she started. "Joseph and I were betrothed, but we had not yet been married. I was working, sweeping the floor of my parents' home."

Katie and Patrick leaned closer, listening to every word Mary said.

"Suddenly, the room was filled with a bright light, and I heard a voice in the room with me. I called for my parents and then for Joseph, but the voice wasn't any of them."

"What did the voice say?" Katie asked. "Who was it?" Even though she'd heard this story so many times before, it was like she was hearing Mary's story for the very first time.

"I turned toward that bright light," Mary answered, "and I heard the words, 'Hail, favored one! The Lord is with you.' Then I saw an angel, standing in the midst of all of that light."

"Then what happened?" Patrick asked. He leaned even closer to Mary.

"I was very afraid!" Mary said, shivering at the memory. "But the angel—Gabriel was his name—told me that I must not fear. And then came the most amazing news. The angel told me that I would conceive a son, and that his name would be Jesus!"

Joseph smiled at the memory, kindly handing Mary the last of the figs.

"But I was confused," Mary went on. "I told the angel that Joseph and I were not yet married, and that I am a virgin. How could this be possible?"

"So, what did Gabriel say?" Katie asked.

"He comforted me, telling me that the Holy Spirit would come upon me and that God's power would overshadow me. He said my son would be called holy, that he would be God's Son!"

"God's Son!" Patrick asked. "Wow."

"The angel then shared happy news with me," Mary continued. "My relative Elizabeth, who is already very old, had also become pregnant! Even though everyone thought that Elizabeth and Zechariah could never have a baby."

"Anything's possible for God," Katie smiled.

"You are right, Katie!" Mary said. "So I told the angel yes! I would serve God. I would be his handmaid. I will do whatever God asks of me, even though I don't understand everything. I will trust."

Mary turned to Joseph. He nodded, "We will trust."

"And then what happened?" Patrick asked.

"I packed a few things, and told Joseph what had happened. He agreed that I must go help," Mary said. "So I set off to travel to the hill country, to care for Elizabeth and her baby!"

▲ Chapter Six ▲

"Elizabeth must have been so happy to see you!" Katie said. "Was she surprised when you got there?"

"Young ones," Joseph said, lifting a hand to pause Mary's story. "The sun has risen. It's time that we begin today's journey if we hope to arrive in Bethlehem tonight."

"What can we do to help?" Patrick asked.

"Patrick," Joseph said in his kind, quiet voice, "please help me pack Nicholas's bags. We have only a few things with us, and our strong donkey is carrying them all, plus Mary."

"I'll put out the fire," Katie offered, "and help Mary get ready."

Both twins jumped into action, more excited than they'd ever been to help with their mom's chore chart at home. Before long, it was time to go. Joseph led them out along the dusty road. Mary sat on Nicholas's back, both legs off to one side. Behind her were blankets, Joseph's simple carpentry tools, and the few other things that Mary and Joseph had packed for their trip. These were tied into small bundles and strapped to Nicholas.

"Nicholas is a strong donkey!" Katie said.

Nicholas's ears perked up when he heard his name.

"Heehaw!" he agreed. Everyone laughed. The twins noticed how carefully Nicholas walked, taking great care to carry Mary gently. The bell around his neck clanged softly.

Patrick took a long turn holding the brown rope of Nicholas's halter. Mary kept them entertained with stories for many miles, but soon fell silent.

"Are you OK?" Katie asked, looking at Mary's belly and imagining the tiny baby inside her.

"Will we make it in time?" Patrick asked Joseph.

"Fear not, young ones," Joseph answered in his quiet way. He looked at the sky, which was now bright in the midday sun.

"You're so calm," Patrick said. "Are you scared? I mean, you're going to be a dad soon!"

Katie shushed her brother, worried that he might upset Mary or Joseph.

"God is with us," Joseph answered with a smile.

"Joseph," Mary said, "why don't you share the story of your dream?"

"Yes!" Katie agreed. "We'd love to hear that story!"

The four walked on for a few moments. The clomping of Nicholas's hooves in the dirt and the clanking of his bell were the only sounds. Then Joseph began to talk.

"I loved Mary very much," Joseph said. "But, when I learned that she had become pregnant, I was very afraid for her and our future."

Katie thought Joseph was so kind and caring with Mary. Even when he looked at Mary's ginormous belly, you could feel his tender love for her.

"I thought maybe I should send Mary away quietly, to protect her and the child. But one night, I had an amazing dream."

"But it was not a dream," Mary said, scratching Nicholas between his perked ears.

"No," Joseph said, "it was the angel."

"What did the angel say?" Patrick asked.

"He told me that I shouldn't be afraid to take Mary into my home as my wife. The angel told me that through the power of the Holy Spirit, Mary would have a baby."

Joseph stopped Nicholas. They stood in the middle of the rocky path to Bethlehem. The sun was beginning to get lower in the sky. It would be night soon.

"The angel said Mary would bear a son. He said that I was to name the child Jesus, because this very special baby would save God's people from their sins."

"Jesus," Joseph repeated, gently touching Mary's stomach. "The voice of the angel was so clear. I knew then what to do. God wants me to protect Mary and baby Jesus. I will spend the rest of my life caring for them, teaching Jesus and watching God's precious child grow."

"So, you see," Mary said, looking down from Nicholas's back. "We have both given God our yes!"

Around them, the twins noticed the landscape changing. Now, lots of other people were traveling the same direction. The dusty path was filled with donkeys and families, all moving together in the tight space. Ahead of them, they saw a little town in the distance.

"Bethlehem!" Patrick said.

"Indeed," said Joseph, looking at the crowds on the road, "we must find a place to stay for the night."

Katie looked at the expression on Mary's face. "And soon!" she said.

▲ Chapter Seven ▲

The road into Bethlehem continued to grow more crowded and noisy. Katie and Patrick saw families large and small with donkeys and goats and other animals. Large oxen with massive horns pulled big wooden carts. The carts overflowed and the donkeys and even the goats were loaded down with people, baskets, and supplies. Suddenly, their quiet path to Bethlehem felt more like the highway back home, with everyone rushing to get to the same place at the same time.

"These crowds concern me," Joseph said. He had been patiently inching Nicholas and Mary forward for the last hour. They were making little progress, and it was getting dark.

"How are you feeling, Mary?" Katie asked. Mary had been quiet for a while.

"A little tired," was all she said.

"Where were you planning to stay?" Patrick asked.

"We hadn't made plans," Joseph answered. "We have some kinsfolk here, but, with so many coming into Bethlehem, we don't know if they will have room for us. We will have to see when we arrive."

"I've got an idea!" Katie offered. "We can't move too quickly with this crowd and Nicholas..."

"And Mary," Patrick continued. He knew exactly what his twin was planning. "But Katie and I could run ahead..."

"And find a place for you," Katie finished. "We could get everything ready!"

"I think this is a very good idea," Joseph said, looking at Mary with worried eyes.

Joseph handed Patrick a few small metal coins, and the twins began their mission. They weaved their way through the oxen and carts and people on the narrow road. Soon, they entered the little town of Bethlehem.

One of the first buildings they saw had an open area in front. Families filled the space, spreading cloths on the ground and gathering around simple meals of bread and dried fish.

"Let's try here," Katie said.

But as soon as they walked up to the old man who was in charge of the inn, he waved them away. "No room!" he shouted impatiently, pointing them to another building down the busy dirt road.

"Pardon me," Patrick said to the next innkeeper, "We are looking for a room for tonight."

"I am sorry," the young woman answered. "We have no rooms. With everyone going to their home town to be counted for the enrollment, there are just so many visitors in our quiet little town!"

Patrick and Katie wandered back onto the dirt road. All around them they heard the sound of families bickering. Everyone was facing the same problem…too many people, and not enough beds.

"What are we going to tell Joseph?" Patrick asked.

"Let's try that place," Katie said, pointing to a dark building near the end of the road. "If we run straight there, maybe we can beat the crowds."

Patrick didn't argue. They both ran as fast as they could, keeping an eye on the crowds to make sure that no one would arrive before them.

"Let's hope they have a place!" Katie panted.

"It doesn't look good," Patrick said, slowing to a jog as they neared the rundown building. "It actually looks pretty creepy."

Katie looked up at the stone building in front of them. It was dark, with only one small wooden door and not a single window. In the doorway, a short man with black hair and eyes was staring at them.

"Maybe we should go back," Katie whispered. "This place is kinda scary."

Patrick looked back at the mass of people lining Bethlehem's main street. Behind them, other families were approaching the dark, depressing little inn. "I think this is our last hope," he said. He threw back his shoulders, standing as tall as he could, and approached the innkeeper.

Katie shivered at the thought of Mary having her baby in this gloomy building, and whispered, "God, please help us find the perfect place for Mary and Joseph!"

▲ Chapter Eight ▲

"Excuse me, sir," Patrick said, his voice trembling. The innkeeper glanced over Patrick's head at another family that was approaching. Katie saw their fancy cart, pulled by four oxen. She watched as the head of the family poured a pile of coins from his leather pouch.

"Sir?" Katie echoed Patrick. "We need a place for our friends Mary and Joseph to stay for tonight."

The innkeeper's eyes were fixed on the rich cart and its owner's bundle of coins. He looked right over the twins' red heads.

"So, can they stay here?" Patrick asked hopefully. In his hand, he had the two small coins Joseph had given him. He feared the worst, knowing that the rich family would probably win a bidding war for the last room in Bethlehem.

"Innkeeper!" boomed the man's voice from behind the twins. "I am in need of your entire inn for my family. I can pay you handsomely."

Katie whirled around to face him. "Hey, we were here first!"

Patrick put his hand on Katie's shoulder, preparing to head back out onto the road to meet Mary and Joseph. *What will we tell them?* he thought. *We couldn't find a place...*

But just as the twins were ready to admit defeat, the innkeeper spoke. "I am sorry, my good man," the man said. "I have only one space to rent out. And I have just promised it to these young ones."

"I will pay you seven times what they have offered!" the rich man argued.

"Try my friend Amir, three doors back," the innkeeper said. "He can usually find a room for a family with a few extra coins." With that, the fancy cart was turned around and the rich family headed back down Bethlehem's main road.

"Thank you!" Katie said, rushing to hug the innkeeper, forgetting that he had seemed strange just minutes before. "Our friend Mary is about to have her baby. We are so grateful that she can stay with you!"

"I will run back to the road and get them," Patrick said, already turning to sprint back to Joseph.

"My young friends," the innkeeper said, stopping Patrick, "first, I must explain myself."

Uh-oh, Katie thought, ready to hear bad news. "Are you going to ask us for more money?" she asked.

"No," the man smiled. "Nothing of the sort. I just need for you to know that this is not a fancy inn like some of the others you have seen. I have only a very small space to give you for this night. In fact, it is normally where my animals live." He pointed to a rock formation next to the tiny building.

"A cave?" Patrick asked, considering the rock opening. Patrick turned to Katie. "I thought we were looking for a stable!"

"It is dry and warm," the innkeeper said. "And it is private. Your friends will have the place to themselves."

"Perfect!" Katie smiled. "Patrick, go get them!"

With that, Patrick turned and sprinted away. He disappeared between the oncoming carts and animals.

Katie turned to the innkeeper. "I'm so sorry; I did not even ask your name, sir! I am Katie. And that," she motioned down the busy road, "was my brother, Patrick. We are so grateful."

"Welcome to Bethlehem, Katie," he answered. "My name is Zadok. Now, let us go to prepare for your friends."

Zadok lit a lantern and called into the cave, "Shalom, my friends!"

Katie heard the mooing of cows, the bleating of goats, and the scratching of a few chickens. "This is a simple place," Zadok said, "but it is quiet and safe."

Katie's eyes settled on a wooden box filled with dirty hay, which sat in the middle of the cave. She recognized it from the many nativity scenes she'd seen in her life. A manger!

She knelt in front of the manger, her hands sifting through the scratchy straw. *We'll have to get some clean hay,* she thought.

Smiling up at the innkeeper, she said, "It's perfect, Zadok!"

▲ Chapter Nine ▲

"Thank you, Katie!" Mary said as she and Joseph entered the small cave.

"It's not very nice," Katie apologized, "but we've tried to clean it up a bit." She waved toward Zadok, who was standing in the corner. He and Katie had spent the last half hour sweeping up animal droppings and whisking the chickens into a pen made of sticks. A cow mooed in the corner, welcoming Mary and Joseph.

"It's perfect," Mary said. She turned to Zadok. "We are so grateful for your hospitality." She rubbed her massive belly.

"You are welcome," Zadok said, "to stay as long as you like. I will leave you now to settle in. Please, come and find me if I can do anything to make your stay more comfortable."

Joseph walked with the innkeeper toward the opening of the cave. He remained silent, but his warm handshake told Zadok how grateful he was.

Patrick looked at Mary. She had grown very quiet again. He could tell that the time for her baby to arrive was coming soon.

"Mary," Katie said, "we made a bed for you here in the corner."

Joseph led Mary to the spot where Katie and Zadok had piled a few thin grey blankets on the dirt floor. Patrick brought the lantern over and clipped it to a hook in the wall. Joseph brought Nicholas into the cave, tethering him next to the cow.

"Thank you for bringing us to Bethlehem safely," he said.

Heehaw, clank, clank. Nicholas bobbed his head.

"Patrick," Katie said, "I think we should go find some clean hay."

"But the baby is coming soon!" Patrick looked nervously at Nicholas's clanking bell. He was definitely not ready to Chime Travel home yet!

Katie insisted, "Zadok told me where we can find fresh hay."

"But what if they need us?"

"What they need," she said sternly, "is clean hay for the manger. Zadok told me that he would send for his mother. She will be here soon to help Mary."

"Thank you for your thoughtfulness, Katie," Joseph said.

As the twins left the cave's rocky opening, Patrick complained, "We're going to miss the whole thing!"

"Patrick," Katie said, stopping her brother, "we're here! It's Christmas night—*the* Christmas night!"

"I know," Patrick confessed. "That's why I don't want to miss anything."

Katie agreed, but knew the couple needed their privacy, too. Her brother reluctantly followed her to where Zadok had instructed her to go.

"I can't believe that Zadok took us in like that…a bunch of strangers," Katie said thoughtfully.

"He is pretty cool. And you're probably right," he said. "They do need clean hay! That hay in the manger looked gnarly. And I think I spotted one of Bernard's mouse cousins sleeping in the bottom of it!"

The twins walked along a small path that led from the cave up a hill and out into an open field. Overhead, the sky was midnight blue. In the distance, the twins spotted a flock of sheep grazing under the full moon. To the side of the path, a stack of fresh hay gleamed in the moonlight.

"Can you believe we're really here?" Katie asked. "Mom's read us this story in our children's Bible a million times!"

"Yeah," Patrick said, piling a handful of hay into a basket. "But, somehow, I thought it would be different…"

"That it wouldn't smell like animals?" Katie giggled.

"Or maybe just that it would be nicer," he said. "You know, like the nativity scene at St. Anne's!"

Katie laughed, thinking how the rocky cave looked nothing like the stable Mr. Danks had built. Then she grinned at her twin. "I told you camels shouldn't be in there yet!"

"Shhh!" Patrick shushed her, suddenly serious. His head whipped back in the direction of the cave. "Did you hear that?"

"Hear what?" Katie asked.

And then she heard it too!

The sound of a tiny baby, crying in the night.

The twins crammed hay into their baskets and ran as fast as they could to see Jesus.

▲ Chapter Ten ▲

"Waaaaa!"

Clank, clank.

Heehaw!

"He's here!" Patrick said over the sound of Nicholas's bell.

"Shhh!" Katie shushed her twin. She fell on her knees at Mary's side. Patrick slid in beside Joseph, his mouth wide open in amazement.

"Baby Jesus!" they said in unison.

"Waaaaa!" the baby cried. His red little face crinkled, covered with tiny tears. Joseph held Mary's hand gently, then wiped her face and offered her a sip of water. Nearby, Zadok's mother, Tamar, unwound long strips of clean white linen.

"I never imagined that he'd cry so loudly!" Patrick said.

Katie remembered how Hoa Hong had screamed when she was tiny. *I guess all babies cry!* she thought. The sight of Mary, so far from her own home and bed, holding her newborn made Katie think of the Perez family and their baby. It must be scary to have a new baby and be so far away from home!

Mary accepted the strips of fabric from Tamar and began twisting them around the baby's little legs and arms, sweeping them up tightly against his body. He made calm, cooing sounds. Mary held him to her chest. Joseph stood by her protectively, smiling at the bundled child.

"He's the cutest baby ever!" Katie said. Patrick nodded, then stood to shake Joseph's hand. It

seemed like something Dad might do at a time like this.

"Hey, Joseph," Patrick said, "Nicholas hasn't been out for a while. Want us to take him for a walk and feed him?"

A few minutes later, Katie and Patrick led the donkey by his tether up into the sheep field. In the distance, they spotted a group of men and boys huddled around a campfire.

"Hey!" Patrick pointed. "Shepherds!"

They hurried toward the crowd. Nicholas followed at a trot, led by his tether rope.

"Hi!" Katie said as the twins and their donkey hurried up to the campfire.

"Who goes there?" one of the older shepherds asked, raising his long, hooked shepherd's staff as a warning. He glanced at his flock, counting them.

"This is my sister, Katie. And I'm…"

As he was introducing himself, Patrick spotted a young boy sitting close to the fire. At his feet was a "ball" made of long strips of black wool, wound around and around.

"Hey," Patrick pointed to the ball, "do you play?"

The boy looked confused for a moment. Patrick gestured to the wool-ball. The boy nodded and smiled. Patrick picked up the ball, and began dribbling it off his feet, knees, and head.

The boy's face lit up. He grabbed the ball in midair and ran, dribbling it to the middle of the pasture. Before long, Patrick, Katie, the shepherd boy and half a dozen other shepherds were playing together under the starry sky.

Suddenly, light appeared above them. The field was as bright as midday.

The head shepherd stopped the impromptu game and squinted up at the source of the light. The twins saw the other shepherds fall into a crowd behind their leader, cowering.

Overhead, a
massive being
hovered in the
sky. It was dressed like
a warrior, in armor like the
old-fashioned knights
wore. But the creature
they saw was dazzling
white and had enormous
wings. An angel!

"Don't be afraid," the
angel's voice boomed. "I proclaim to you good
news of great joy that will be for all the people!"

"It's Gabriel!" Katie said to Patrick. Between
them, Nicholas trembled under the bright light.

Patrick shielded his green eyes. Next to him,
the shepherd boy's eyes were wide with wonder.

"For today," the booming voice continued, "in
the city of David a Savior has been born for you
who is Messiah and Lord."

"Emmanuel!" Katie whispered. Nearby, the shepherds were beginning to stand up in awe.

"And this will be a sign for you: You will find an infant wrapped in swaddling clothes and lying in a manger."

Patrick watched as thousands of bright lights began to fill the midnight sky. Each began as a tiny speck, expanding to reveal more and more hovering angels.

All at once, the angels' voices rose together. "Glory to God in the highest," they shouted over and over. "And on earth peace to those on whom his favor rests!"

Their cries echoed for several minutes. Then the sound ended in an instant. The sky went dark again. Silence rang in the twins' ears. After a stunned moment, everyone began to look at one another, the angels' news sinking in.

"Do you want to see the baby?" Patrick asked.

"Let us go!" the head shepherd answered, "to Bethlehem to see what the Lord has made known to us."

"Follow us!" Patrick said.

"We'll show you the way!" Katie nodded.

With that, two redheaded twins, a grey donkey, the shepherd boy and his wool ball, several men, and a flock full of sheep ran toward town, beneath the star-filled sky.

▲ Chapter Eleven ▲

It didn't take long for the ragtag group to arrive at the cave where Mary, Joseph, and Jesus were resting.

"I'm not sure how Mary and Joseph are going to feel," Katie said to Patrick, "about all of these strangers tromping into the cave with a newborn baby!"

"Something makes me think that they'll be OK with it," Patrick laughed.

A riot of noise filled the air with Nicholas's bell clanking, the sheep baaaing and the shepherds arguing about who would be first to see the newborn king.

"We have awaited the coming of the Messiah for many years," Ra'ah, the head shepherd, told Katie and Patrick. "Now that the king has come, my greatest hope has come true." Ra'ah held the hand of his young son, David. Across his shoulders, David held a baby sheep.

"A gift," David said to Patrick, "for the king! This is Bessie, my first ewe."

Patrick smiled down at him. The shepherd boy was hardly bigger than the lamb he held. Patrick thought of that troublemaking Perez boy and realized with regret that he hadn't even asked the boy's name!

"You may present Bessie to the king," Ra'ah said to David, "but remember your manners!"

Patrick knocked politely on the rock at the opening of the cave, calling into Joseph. "Joseph, Mary? We brought a few new friends who wanted to see your baby."

"Of course," Joseph welcomed from inside the cave. "Please, join us and share our joy."

Patrick and Katie stood by the cave's opening, watching as the shepherds piled into the small space. The smell of sheep mixed with the odor of the cows and chickens. Joseph led Nicholas by his tether, loosely tying him near the manger. Patrick noticed how protectively the donkey watched the baby, especially as the noisy sheep began to fill the corners of the cave.

"Maybe we should tell some of them to wait outside," Katie suggested to Mary. "We didn't realize how many were coming! But when they saw the angels and heard their message, they were all so excited!"

"They are all welcome, Katie," Mary said. Even though she looked tired, she was smiling down on little baby Jesus asleep in the clean hay that the twins had laid for him in the animals' feeding box.

"Excuse me, my lady," little David said to Mary. He wiggled his way through the crowd of older shepherds and stood in front of the manger, holding Bessie. "I have a present for the king. This is Bessie. She is the best lamb of all. Her coat will keep the king warm!"

"Why, thank you, young one!" Joseph said, accepting Bessie from David. Patrick noticed the tears that formed in David's eyes as the weight of the lamb was lifted from his arms.

"What is your name, young shepherd?" Mary asked.

"David, my lady," he answered.

"David," Mary said, pointing at baby Jesus. "You have given our son his first gift! We are so grateful for your generosity! Bessie will be Jesus's first playmate."

As if to agree with Mary, the baby awoke from his sleep and smiled up into the face of the shepherd boy. David knelt in front of the manger, holding the baby's fingers with awe.

Over the next several minutes, the cave was a swirl of activity. Each of the shepherds took a turn bowing and kneeling in front of the wooden manger. Mary and Joseph watched and listened, smiling the whole time. Finally, tall Ra'ah took his turn to come before the baby and honor him.

"God's peace is now upon us," Ra'ah said to Mary and Joseph, "for we have witnessed the coming of God's anointed one."

"We thank you for coming," Joseph said. "We are grateful for your gifts and for little Bessie."

"Yeah!" Katie agreed, "and for all of the food you left for us, and the firewood and wool blankets!"

"We came here with nothing," Patrick nodded, "and you gave us this great welcome. How can we ever thank you?"

"We thank you," said Ra'ah, "for giving us the joy of being with you on this most holy of nights.

We will never forget what we have seen and heard!"

David ran to the twins, hugging them good-bye.

Patrick smiled. "Don't worry; we'll take good care of Bessie."

The shepherds left, buzzing with excitement about Jesus, the newborn king. They piled out of the cave and rushed toward the streets of Bethlehem, anxious to tell everyone what they had seen.

▲ Chapter Twelve ▲

When the cave was finally clear of sheep and shepherds, Patrick and Katie used some of the extra hay to make a bed of their own. Little Bessie tucked in between them, bleating contentedly. Nicholas stood nearby, watching over the cave as silence fell. Mary gazed at her precious Son, pondering everything that had happened.

Over the next few days, Patrick and Katie fell into a routine with Mary, Joseph, and baby Jesus. They helped them out during the days, cooking meals, taking care of Nicholas, and running errands. At night, Jesus would wake a few times to be fed by Mary. One night, his loud crying awakened the twins. After a while, it was clear that nothing could make little Jesus happy.

"May I try holding him?" Katie asked Mary. "I used to swaddle my little sister Hoa Hong when she first came to live with us. I was pretty good at it!"

Mary nodded and held Jesus out to her. His little face was bright red and damp with tears. Katie cradled him close, gently tucking his wool

blanket tighter, and started walking in circles and humming. Before long, the baby's screams quieted, and he was soon asleep in her arms. After that night, Mary would invite Katie to cuddle Jesus to sleep after his feedings.

Each morning, Katie and Patrick swept the cave, collected

fresh hay for Jesus's manger, helped Zadok feed the animals, and took Nicholas for a walk in Bethlehem. The sleepy little village began to feel like home as they visited stalls to buy fruit or fish. Katie learned whom to ask for the best prices, and Patrick became an expert at cooking over an open fire.

"Thank you for all you are doing to help us!" Mary said to Patrick and Katie one day as she was feeding baby Jesus. "It's very hard to be so far away from my parents. Having you here with us makes Bethlehem feel more like home."

Katie smiled, then looked away quickly. She rushed outside, making an excuse about Nicholas needing some fresh air.

Patrick followed her. He could easily track Katie by the sound of Nicholas's bell.

"Hey," he called out as he ran up to her, "is something wrong?"

"I've just been thinking," Katie said, "about the Perez family. Mr. and Mrs. Perez are a little bit like Mary and Joseph…"

"Yeah," Patrick nodded, "far away from home and family. Without any of their stuff. And at Christmas!"

Katie stopped along the path, lightly petting Nicholas's mane. "They're surrounded by strangers," she said.

"And none of us have been very nice to them," Patrick admitted. "We weren't exactly welcoming."

Katie turned Nicholas around on the path and stared back at the cave. "How long do you think we'll be here?" she asked.

"I have no idea," Patrick answered. "I guess long enough to figure out what this mission is all about…but it's been eight whole days since Jesus was born."

They talked quietly about what they remembered from the story of Jesus's birth in the Bible. They wondered if they'd get to meet the wise men or go to Jerusalem with the family to visit the Temple. As they made their way back to the stable, both of them were thinking the same thing: I hope we get to see it all!

▲ Chapter Thirteen ▲

"Today is the day we go to the Temple in Jerusalem," Joseph said one morning before dawn. "We will leave early. The walk will take us a few hours."

"Is Nicholas coming?" Patrick asked.

"Of course!" Joseph answered. *Heehaw!* echoed the donkey.

Mary and Katie packed simple meals for them to eat, and before long it was time to begin the walk to Jerusalem. "We go for the purification, a special ritual for new mothers," Mary explained, "and to present Jesus in the Temple."

The twins' excitement g
mile, and when they final
horizon early that aftern
The Temple was huge an
of a hill like a king on a

The streets of Jerusa
people at stalls selling a variety of things. The
stalls closest to the Temple sold small lambs and
different types of birds. Joseph stopped at one
of the stands. When he returned from the bird
salesman, Joseph handed Patrick a cage made of
bent branches.

"Turtledoves," he said.

Patrick looked at the grey birds
flapping their wings inside the cage.
"What are they for?"

"For the Temple gift," Joseph
answered. "Be very careful with
them."

Soon it w
big whit
In fa
to

...s time to enter the Temple. But the ...e building was not like St. Anne's at all. ...t, most parts of the Temple were open only ... men, with some parts reserved only to the high priests.

Mary and Joseph tied Nicholas up outside and climbed the white steps with baby Jesus. Near the opening of the Temple, an old man came toward them.

"Praise be to God!" the man said as he looked at the baby. His hands shook with excitement. Katie could tell that, although he was very old, he was also very holy. He had long white hair, and his face was pale with excitement.

Joseph introduced himself. "This is Mary, and our baby is…"

"I am Simeon," the man interrupted. "And this…this is the child!" He waved his gnarled fingers at baby Jesus, then began pointing between the infant and the sky. Simeon fell to his knees, giving thanks to God and kissing the floor of the Temple. Katie and Patrick exchanged an amazed look. How did this man know who Jesus was?

Simeon turned toward Mary and Joseph, his eyes filled with tears. "I never believed this day would truly come! I have seen my Lord," he said. "Now, I can die in peace!"

▲ Chapter Fourteen ▲

"Die in peace?" Patrick whispered to his sister. "Right now? Here?!"

Katie punched him in the ribs. "Shhhh!"

Joseph helped Simeon stand upright and then placed Jesus into the old man's arms. Simeon held him close. Looking up to heaven, the man began to pray out loud, tears streaming down his face.

"Now, Master, you may let your servant go in peace, according to your word. For my eyes have seen this child—your son! Jesus."

Handing the baby back to Joseph, Simeon spoke quietly to the babe's parents. He gestured wildly as he spoke, telling them about things that would happen in Jesus's life. Mary and Joseph listened, amazed at what the old man was saying.

"How can he know so much?" Patrick asked Katie. "Jesus is only a baby."

"God must have told him," Katie answered. "Look at him. Simeon's such a holy man!"

After talking with Mary and Joseph for several minutes, Simeon gave the family a special blessing. He turned to Mary and looked into her eyes.

"This child of yours," he said to her, "is very special. It is his destiny to be the rise and fall of many in Israel. He is a sign of God's love for all of us."

Mary nodded, gazing down at her son.

"But you…," Simeon continued, "this will be very hard for you, Mary. You will feel like your heart is being pierced with a sword, but you must be strong. Through Jesus, many hearts will be turned to God!"

Mary bravely accepted Simeon's words.

"Why is he saying this stuff to her?" Katie asked. "What if he's scaring her?"

"Mary's amazing!" Patrick said. "She can handle this. Look at her." The twins watched as Mary and Joseph respectfully thanked Simeon. Mary showed no sign of the fear. She bowed before the old man as Joseph presented the turtledoves.

After the family left Simeon, they went into the Temple to complete the different ceremonies required. Katie and Patrick were able to follow them, and silently observed everything with wonder. The Jewish traditions were unfamiliar to them, but they could feel God's presence in this holy place. Throughout everything, baby Jesus calmly looked around with wide, alert eyes, almost as if he understood the importance of what was happening.

Finally, the ceremonies were over, and it was time to go. As they passed through the Court of Women, an elderly woman with deeply wrinkled

skin and bright eyes turned her face toward them. She was resting on a mat. Around her were simple bits of food, a small basket, and a tiny blanket.

"It looks like she lives here!" Patrick said to Katie.

As they passed, the woman struggled to stand up from her straw mat.

"She's ancient!" Katie whispered.

But even as the twins were hoping that they could get away before the strange old lady reached them, Mary turned and greeted her.

"Praise be to God," the old lady said to Mary. "I am Anna, daughter of Phanuel. I have waited for this day for many years."

Behind Anna, a younger woman came up, helping to steady her so she wouldn't fall from excitement.

"Anna is here day and night," the young woman said. "Ever since her husband died many years ago, she lives here in the Temple. She is continually praying and fasting."

Anna spent a long time talking to Mary and Joseph about little Jesus. When it was time for them to leave the Temple, Anna gave Mary a hug. "Thanks be to God," she said, her voice raspy with emotion. "I have met him! And now I will tell everyone!"

As Mary, Joseph, Jesus, and the twins were making their way toward the Temple stairs, they heard Anna's voice echo behind them.

"Come over here! I must tell you about this child I have met today. He has come to save all of Jerusalem!"

Katie looked back and saw a crowd gathering around the old woman. From her seat on her straw mat, Anna began to tell anyone who would listen the story of Jesus's birth.

▲ Chapter Fifteen ▲

The days were busy for Patrick and Katie, filled with normal things like buying and cooking food, taking care of Nicholas and Bessie and the other animals, and helping out with chores for Mary and Joseph.

"It's sort of like our chores at home," Katie said one day, several weeks after their visit to the Temple. "But here, they take five times longer."

"I know," Patrick agreed, "I never thought I'd miss a vacuum cleaner so much!"

Little Jesus grew bigger every day. He learned to roll over, to sit up, and to crawl. Suddenly, the twins had to be careful about where they left things so that Jesus wouldn't find them and put them in his mouth. He was a busy baby, into everything!

"I remember when Hoa Hong was this age!" Patrick said.

"Do you miss her?" Katie asked.

"I do," he answered, "but it's so cool being here."

"I know," Katie said. "There's not much in the Bible about this stuff, the regular kind of stuff that happened when Jesus was a kid."

"Their family's a lot like ours," Patrick said, pointing to Mary, who was preparing lunch. Nearby, Joseph was working on a carpentry project. "Everybody's got a job to do."

"You're better about doing your jobs here than at home!" Katie teased. They'd both enjoyed life with Mary, Joseph, and Jesus. They didn't even miss their Tunebuddies or Master Blaster games. They loved stories around the cooking fire, games, and playing with baby Jesus. Joseph often led them in prayer. Mary was always busy with Jesus, but had become like a mom to the twins, too.

One evening, as Mary was getting ready to put Jesus to bed, Nicholas began braying outside.

Heehaw!

Clank, clank.

"What is he upset about?" Katie asked.

Patrick and Joseph went outside to investigate. For some reason, the night seemed brighter than usual. They looked up and saw a star. It was so bright that they had to cover their eyes against its glare.

"What is that?" Katie asked.

Before they could answer, they heard the sound of approaching animals. A band of men on camels came riding up to them from out of the darkness. The camels were huge and loaded with all sorts of packages and bundles. Patrick saw not only men, but also some teenage boys who looked like servants. There were three main leaders, each riding a camel and wearing luxurious and colorful fabrics.

"We have come," said one of the leaders, "to see the newborn king of the Jews." He jumped off his camel and extended his hand to Joseph. "We saw the king's star at its rising."

"And we have followed it here across many miles," said another. "We have come to pay homage to this king!"

"Homage?" Patrick asked Katie. "Is that the money they use here?"

"No, stupid!" Katie whispered. "These must be the wise men! They came to give gifts to Jesus!"

"You mean the three kings?"

"Yeah!"

Joseph welcomed them all.

They had traveled many miles from Persia. "At home," the leader said, "we are Magi. We study the stars. This one led us to you!" He pointed to the bright star, which now seemed to be hovering directly over them.

"Along the way," he continued, "we met with your King Herod. He asked that we return to him once we met the child to tell him where he can find you. He wants to come visit, too, to honor the king."

A worried look crossed Joseph's face, but he still welcomed the strangers. "Please," Joseph said, "you have traveled many miles. We welcome you!" He led the three Magi into the house, where Mary held Jesus in her arms.

▲ Chapter Sixteen ▲

The Magi piled inside the small living space joyfully. With their fancy clothes and servants, they seemed to fill every corner with color and spicy smells. Their camels stayed outside with Nicholas.

As soon as the men saw little Jesus in Mary's arms, they hurried to him. One by one, they lay face-down on the floor in front of the baby. Katie and Patrick watched as they stayed still, flat on the floor, for several minutes.

"Are they OK?" Katie asked.

"I think they are showing their respect," Patrick whispered.

"Mary, are you sure you want all of these strangers around the baby?" Katie asked.

Mary smiled at Katie. "These men are no more strangers than the shepherds were. They came all this way to meet Jesus. Strangers are simply new friends, just waiting to be loved."

When the Magi stood up, they called to their servants forward with bundles of gifts. Each of the three Magi took a turn presenting his gift to Jesus.

"Precious gold," said the first as he opened a small trunk revealing golden coins, "A gift fit for a king."

The second brought forward a clay jar. When he opened it and said, "Frankincense," a sweet smell filled the room.

"It smells like lemons, combined with a Christmas tree!" Patrick whispered.

The third wise man came forward with a jar of gleaming oil. "Myrrh," he said, as he presented his gift to Jesus, who smiled at its shiny color.

The Magi were enthralled by the babe. "We've traveled far to pay tribute to the king," the leader said. "We were planning to tell King Herod how to find this place, too."

The second king interrupted him. "But last night, we were warned in a dream that this was not the right thing to do."

"In fact," the third said, "we must warn you. It seems that King Herod is greatly troubled by the birth of this new king."

Joseph and Mary looked at each other. They knew in their hearts that Jesus was not an ordinary baby. It seemed Herod knew it, too.

"It is not safe for you to remain here," the head Magi said. "We have decided not to return to Herod in Jerusalem. We will take a different route home. Herod will not learn from us where to find the king."

Katie listened to the Magi's warnings and shivered. Suddenly, Jesus, Mary, and Joseph were not safe in their own home. But where could they go?

After the three kings left, Mary and Joseph spoke quietly together. "We need not fear," Joseph said. "God will protect us."

His words were a comfort to Mary and the baby, who fell asleep quickly. But both Patrick and Katie were restless, tossing and turning. Were the Magi really new friends, or strangers looking to hurt Jesus? In their hearts, they knew the answer.

In the middle of the night, Joseph woke suddenly. He lit the lantern, and Mary stirred.

Patrick and Katie heard him say, "The angel just came to me in a dream."

"What did the angel say, Joseph?" Mary asked.

"He told me, 'Rise, take the child and his mother, flee to Egypt, and stay there until I tell you.'"

Turning to the twins, Joseph said, "He said that Herod is trying to find Jesus…to destroy him!"

"To destroy him?" Katie said. "We need to get you out of here, now!"

"Yeah!" echoed Patrick. "Now!"

The twins spent the next hour helping Mary and Joseph pack up. Patrick tied bundles of supplies to Nicholas's back. Katie helped Mary climb on top of him and handed baby Jesus to her. Joseph secured Bessie to Nicholas's halter.

"I'll run ahead to check the roads," Patrick said.

"And I'll close up the house," Katie said, "so no one will know that we're gone!"

Joseph led them through the darkness out toward the main dirt road.

"What will happen in Egypt?" Katie asked. "Where will we stay?"

"What will we eat?" Patrick wondered.

Mary smiled serenely. "God will protect us," she said. "We have the Magi's gifts. Egypt may be a land of strangers now, but, when we arrive, I know the strangers will become new friends who will help us."

Patrick looked at Katie, and knew they were thinking the same thing.

"Strangers are new friends, just waiting to be loved," Katie whispered.

Behind them, loud voices shattered the quiet night.

"They are escaping!" a man yelled.

"Hurry! Get them! King Herod orders it!" shouted another.

Joseph grabbed Nicholas's tether. "We are going to have to run! Hold Jesus tightly, Mary!"

Everyone ran as fast as they could, away from the town and toward Egypt. Nicholas's bell clanged with each step he took.

Heehaw!

Clank, clank.

Breathless from running, Patrick and Katie felt the road beneath their feet begin to rumble. A blast of cold wind blew the dirt on the path into swirling circles.

Heehaw!

Clank, clank.

Katie reached for her brother's hand. "Oh, no!" she cried.

Nicholas brayed wildly and his bell rang out a third time.

Heehaw!

Clank, clank.

And suddenly, everything became a blur.

▲ Chapter Seventeen ▲

When the ground finally stopped rumbling, Patrick and Katie opened their eyes and found themselves on their knees in front of the St. Anne's nativity scene.

"...Faithful, joyful and triumphant, O, come ye, o, come ye to Bethlehem..." The silver bells of the choir rang out the traditional tune.

Patrick was at the feet of the camel statue. Katie grasped the donkey figurine.

"We're back!" they said together. In their excitement to hug each other, neither realized that Fr. Miguel was watching them with a smile.

"I need a drink of water," Patrick said, noticing the priest.

Katie answered, "I'm thirsty too. We'll be right back, Father!"

The twins hurried toward the water fountain in the narthex. Seeing that no one else was around, they fist-bumped excitedly.

"We did it!" Katie whispered.

"Together!" Patrick agreed. "It was real, right? We Chime Traveled…"

"To Bethlehem!" Katie finished his sentence. "Wow, we were there for the first Christmas!"

"I'm worried about Mary and Joseph and Jesus," Patrick confessed. "I hope Herod doesn't catch them!"

"Of course he doesn't, silly!" Katie said. "We've read it in the Bible a million times."

"But it was scarier in real life," Patrick said. "What will they do when they get there? How long will they have to stay in Egypt?"

"Try not to worry," Katie assured her brother. "We'll read about it again in the children's Bible when we get home. But for now, I think we have a mission to take care of."

"Right. Some strangers that are new friends…" Patrick started.

"Just waiting to be loved," Katie finished.

At that moment, Sr. Margaret entered the narthex with the Perez family and Fr. Miguel.

"Padre, how do you say, 'Hi, my name is' in Spanish?" Patrick asked.

Fr. Miguel smiled. "*¡Hola! Me llamo Miguel.*"

Patrick offered his hand to Mr. Perez and did his best to repeat the words, "*¡Hola! Me llamo Patrick.*" Then he pointed at Katie. "And this is my sister Katie."

Fr. Miguel whispered something in Katie's ear, and she came forward. "*¡Bienvenido!* Welcome to St. Anne's," she said.

The boy who had been hiding in the manger earlier pushed himself in front of the twins. "*Me llamo Mateo!*" he said. Then he pointed to his baby sister and smiled, "*Y esta es Isabel!*"

Then Mateo pulled his precious toy from his pocket and held it up. "*Y mi burro!*"

"Mateo and Isabel!" Katie smiled, "and, of course, Burro!"

"Burro," Patrick said, pointing to Mateo's toy. "Donkey!"

"Don-key?" Mateo repeated. Patrick nodded. "Donkey!"

Katie asked Fr. Miguel how to say a few more words in Spanish and wished Mr. and Mrs. Perez a merry Christmas. She asked about their family and learned that they had come from very far away and had no family in the area. Because of violence in their country, they had been forced to flee their farmland in the middle of the night.

The governor and many kind people had helped them to find their way to St. Anne's. This would be their first Christmas away from home.

"They came to us with only the clothes on their backs," Fr. Miguel said.

"We want to help," Patrick said. "Here, take this!" He pulled off his green hoodie and wrapped it around Mateo. The little boy grinned.

Katie took her own pink hoodie from around her shoulders and handed it to Mrs. Perez. "For Isabel," she said, "to use as a blanket…"

Mr. and Mrs. Perez accepted the gift, smiling as they swaddled their baby in the pink hoodie. Behind them, Grandpa Perez, "*Abuelo*" as Fr. Miguel had said to call him, nodded his head.

"OK, team," Sr. Margaret said to the Perez family, "it's time we set off for Catholic Charities before they close."

"Will they be at Mass tonight for Christmas Eve?" Katie asked.

"Definitely," Sr. Margaret answered.

"See you tonight," the twins said as Sr. Margaret led the family toward the parish's van.

▲ Chapter Eighteen ▲

Later that day, the kids held the Brady family's children's Bible, taking turns reading verse by verse.

When Herod died, an angel of the Lord suddenly appeared in a dream to Joseph in Egypt and said, "Get up, take the child and his mother, and go to the land of Israel, for those who were seeking the child's life are dead."

Then Joseph got up, took the child and his mother, and went to the land of Israel. But when he heard that Archelaus was ruling over Judea in place of his father Herod, he was afraid to go there. And after being warned in a dream, he went away to the district of Galilee. There he made his home in a town called Nazareth, so that what had been spoken through the prophets might be fulfilled, "He will be called a Nazorean." (Matthew 2:19–23)

"So that's how they got back safely to Nazareth!" Patrick said, closing the cover to the Bible.

Katie nodded. "Thank goodness!"

"We've read it before," he said, "but now it isn't just a story. It's a memory!"

Mrs. Brady was setting the dinner table with the fancy Christmas dishes. Behind her, Dr. Brady was tucking wrapped Christmas presents beneath the Bradys' Christmas tree. The tree was covered with homemade ornaments and strings of popcorn.

"Can we get to Mass early?" Katie asked as she helped Mrs. Brady finish setting the table.

"Yeah," Patrick said from the corner where he was helping Dr. Brady with the tree, "we want to get there before it's too crowded."

"Ewly!" Hoa Hong yelled.

"Well, then, early it is," Dr. Brady smiled.

A few hours later, when they pulled into the St. Anne's parking lot, it was already almost full.

"Lots of families come at Christmas who haven't been with us for the rest of the year. Church will be busy tonight," Mrs. Brady said.

From their seats in the front pew, the twins had a good view of the side of the nativity scene. "Can we take Hoa Hong and go see it?" Katie asked her dad.

"Sure," he said. "Just be sure she doesn't break anything."

"And, Patrick, you don't have your frog, do

you?" their mom teased.

The twins pointed out the different animals to their sister, who giggled and repeated them.

"That stable thing isn't really right," Patrick whispered. "It doesn't look anything like our cave!"

"I know," said Katie. "But at least Fr. Miguel has Nicholas in the right place." She smiled as she looked at the donkey standing protectively by the manger. Near him, a small shepherd boy held a lamb across his shoulders.

"David and Bessie!" Patrick said, pointing.

Hoa Hong pointed to the empty manger. "No baby!" she said.

"That's right, Rosie," Patrick said, calling his sister by her nickname. "It's Christmas Eve. Baby Jesus will come tonight at midnight Mass."

"We'd better head back," Katie whispered. "It's getting pretty crowded."

As they walked to their pew, the twins noticed

Sr. Margaret enter with the Perez family. They searched for an open spot, but every pew was full.

Katie whispered into her mom's ear. Mrs. Brady smiled and nodded, and Katie walked over to Abuelo Perez. She took the man's wrinkled hand and led him to her spot in the pew. Behind her, Patrick invited Mrs. Perez and Isabel to take his seat. Then Patrick took little Mateo's hand and led him to a small space in the pew between the two adults. There was just enough room!

Patrick and Katie stood along the wall with Sr. Margaret and Mr. Perez as the bell choir began the first chimes of "O, Come, All Ye Faithful." Fr. Miguel processed down the aisle, and Christmas Eve Mass began.

▲ Chapter Nineteen ▲

Christmas Eve Mass was a bit longer than a usual Sunday, but with all of the decorations, beautiful Christmas carols, and everyone dressed in their holiday best, Patrick and Katie didn't even notice. After Mass, they asked to take Hoa Hong to see the nativity one more time.

As the three Brady kids were kneeling in front of the crèche, Fr. Miguel approached with the Perez family.

"What are you doing tonight, Padre?" Patrick asked.

"We're headed back to my place," the priest answered. "I'm going to see what I have around to fix us for dinner."

"Oooh," Katie said. "Can you come over to our house with Mateo and Isabel and their family?"

"Yeah!" Patrick said. "We always have pizza on Christmas Eve. It's a Brady family tradition."

"Check with your parents," Fr. Miguel said. "If it's OK with them, we'd love to join you!"

"Gracias," Mr. Perez said after Fr. Miguel shared the twins' invitation.

Patrick and Katie took Hoa Hong by the hand and made their way through the crowded church to their parents.

"Mom, can the Perez family come over for Christmas Eve pizza?" Katie asked.

"And Fr. Miguel, too?" Patrick begged.

"I don't know kids," Dr. Brady said. "This is sort of a last-minute thing to throw on your mom's to-do list."

"But Mom," Katie said. "They are all alone in a new place."

"Yeah, we don't want them to be lonely. And it's Christmas!" Patrick picked up. "Plus, you don't want them to have to eat Fr. Miguel's cooking!"

Mrs. Brady laughed. "OK," she said. "Go find out what kind of pizza is Mateo's favorite."

"Thanks, Mom!" the twins said. Hurrying back to the nativity scene, they made arrangements with Fr. Miguel.

An hour later, the Brady family was back at home. The twins added a card table to the dining room and quickly found extra dishes and silverware. Patrick cleared room for Mateo to play and found a few baby toys of Hoa Hong's for Isabel. Katie pulled the old crib into the dining room, putting it in the corner near the table.

"It's going to be pretty crowded in here tonight," Dad said.

"But, Daddy," Katie answered, "this is the best kind of crowd!"

"I'm surprised that you two want a bunch of strangers over on Christmas Eve. We started doing pizza when you guys were little because you couldn't wait to get to your presents. Having the Perez family here will be nice, but it probably means we're going to be late with unwrapping presents."

Patrick had been organizing his old wooden train set nearby. "Know what strangers are, Dad?" he asked, grinning at Katie.

"What?" Mr. Brady asked.

"They're new friends, just waiting to be loved!" the twins said together.

▲ Chapter Twenty ▲

The doorbell rang, and everyone welcomed the Perez family and Fr. Miguel. Sr. Margaret had come along too, so Mom pulled one more chair up to the table. Both twins laughed when Abuelo Perez tried pepperoni pizza for the first time. Katie held Isabel while Mrs. Perez ate, snuggling her close and thinking how Isabel's head smelled just like baby Jesus's.

After dinner, they all moved out to the living room. Dr. Brady made a fire, and the children gathered around the tree.

Mateo tugged on Patrick's sleeve and spoke in Spanish.

"Um, Padre?" Patrick asked. "Can you tell me what he's saying?"

Katie listened in, still holding baby Isabel.

"He says," Fr. Miguel translated, "that he has a gift for you."

"A gift?" Patrick asked. "For me?"

Patrick was embarrassed for a moment. "But… he doesn't have anything…and I…" Patrick looked at the Christmas tree, where beautiful presents waited to be unwrapped.

"Take it, Patrick," Katie whispered. "You'll make him so happy! Remember David?"

Patrick smiled at Mateo. The boy's face lit up. He offered Patrick a single present, wrapped in brown paper from a used grocery bag. When Patrick accepted it, Mateo's brown eyes beamed with joy.

"What could this be?" Patrick smiled. He sat on the floor next to Mateo. "Will you help me open it?"

Together, they ripped away the brown paper.

When the paper was opened, Patrick was surprised.

"Burro?" he asked Mateo. "But he's your favorite toy!"

"For you!" Mateo said, in lilting English. He pushed the toy donkey into Patrick's arms. "For you!"

"It's the best present anyone's ever given me," Patrick grinned. "I love it!" He hugged Burro close.

Then Mateo turned to Katie. He led her toward Mrs. Perez. Mateo's mom reached into another brown bag and gave something to Mateo. He smiled and handed Katie a beautiful pink rose. "¡Para ti!"

"Oh, Mateo," Katie said, hugging him. "¡*Gracias*! I love it! My favorite kind of flower!"

After everyone was done admiring the gifts, Katie asked if they could read the Christmas story.

"That's a great idea, honey," Mrs. Brady answered.

Patrick and Katie took turns reading from the first few chapters of Luke's Gospel, with Fr. Miguel quietly translating the Bible story into Spanish. When it was finished, Patrick and Katie showed Hoa Hong and Mateo the Brady's nativity scene. The "stable" was made from a shoebox the twins had decorated in kindergarten. The figurines were plastic, and their paint was chipped from years of being handled.

Patrick and Katie remembered the shepherds and wise men who had come to be with baby Jesus. They could still smell the hay and hear the shouts of angels.

The twins looked down at the donkey statue in their nativity. They'd seen it and held it a million times. Now, they were surprised to see a tiny little gold bell tied around the donkey's neck. It had never been there before! They looked at each other.

Suddenly, even though no one was touching it, the golden donkey bell began to ring.

Clank, clank.

"*Heehaw!*" the twins laughed in unison.

The Real Christmas Story

In those days a decree went out from Emperor Augustus that all the world should be registered. This was the first registration and was taken while Quirinius was governor of Syria. All went to their own towns to be registered. Joseph also went from the town of Nazareth in Galilee to Judea, to the city of David called Bethlehem, because he was descended from the house and family of David. He went to be registered with Mary, to whom he was engaged and who was expecting a child. While they were there, the time came for her to deliver her child. And she gave birth to her firstborn son and wrapped him in bands of cloth, and laid him in a manger, because there was no place for them in the inn.

In that region there were shepherds living in the fields, keeping watch over their flock by night. Then an angel of the Lord stood before them, and the glory of the Lord shone around them, and they were terrified. But the angel said to them, "Do not be afraid; for see—I am bringing you good news of great joy for all the people: to you is born this day in the city of David a Savior, who is the Messiah, the Lord. This will be a sign for you: you will find a child wrapped in bands of cloth and lying in a manger." And suddenly there was with the angel a multitude of the heavenly host, praising God and saying,

"Glory to God in the highest heaven,
and on earth peace among those whom he favors!"

When the angels had left them and gone into heaven, the shepherds said to one another, "Let us go now to Bethlehem and see this thing that has taken place, which the Lord has made known to us." So they went with haste and found Mary and Joseph, and the child lying in the manger. When they saw this, they made known what had been told them about this child; and all who heard it were amazed at what the shepherds told them. But Mary treasured all these words and pondered them in her heart. The shepherds returned, glorifying and praising God for all they had heard and seen, as it had been told them.

—Luke 2:1–20, *New Revised Standard Version* (NRSV)

Discussion Questions

1. Patrick and Katie notice a new family at St. Anne's but feel uncomfortable around them at first. How do you feel around people you've never met before? What are some safe and kind ways to make them feel welcome?

2. Patrick and Katie are preoccupied on their way to help clean and set up St. Anne's for the Christmas Eve Mass. What are some things that keep your family busy during the Christmas season and around other holidays or celebrations?

3. Mary and Joseph describe how they gave God their "yes" even though they were uncertain and afraid. What should you do when you feel God calling you to do something special in your life?

4. Even though Patrick and Katie knew the story of the nativity, and that Jesus was to be born in a stable, they still looked anxiously for a safe place for the Holy Family—something that is captured in a unique way in the Mexican tradition of *Las Posadas*. What do you know about this tradition—is this something you could try with your family?

5. If you were in the field with the shepherds, how do you imagine you might have felt when the angels came to announce the good news of Jesus's birth?

6. Little David, the shepherd boy, brings baby Jesus a special present. What gift would you bring to the Christ child if you were there at the manger?

7. Simeon and Anna greet Jesus with great joy, and Anna can't wait to tell everyone about the Messiah. How do you feel when you talk with someone about Jesus? How do you learn more about Jesus?

8. Mary calls strangers, "new friends, just waiting to be loved." How can you be kind to new students at your school or church, or to new neighbors?

9. What is the lesson that Patrick and Katie learn before they can Chime Travel back to St. Anne's?

10. The Brady family invites the Perez family to celebrate Christmas Eve in their home. What are some little ways that you can offer kindness and love to others who might need some extra care?

ABOUT THE AUTHOR

Lisa M. Hendey is the founder and editor of CatholicMom.com and the bestselling author of *The Grace of Yes, The Handbook for Catholic Moms,* and *A Book of Saints for*  *Catholic Moms.* Serving as editor-at-large with Ave Maria Press, Lisa's partnership with Ave has resulted in the CatholicMom.com book imprint, which recently published its ninth book in the series aimed at supporting and uplifting women in their vocations. The five books in the Chime Travelers fiction series for elementary school readers, based upon the lives of the saints, are being read in Catholic elementary schools and homes nationwide.

Hendey has traveled worldwide with and written about the work of Catholic Relief Services and Unbound to support their humanitarian missions. She maintains a busy travel schedule, speaking and giving workshops on faith, family, and Catholic technology and communications topics. But she especially loves to hear from Chime Traveler readers (#chimetravelers). For more information about her "virtual" or in-person author visits, or to find additional teacher's resources and activities about the books, go to www.ChimeTravelerKids.com or contact her directly at lisa@catholicmom.com.

About the Illustrator

Jenn Bower is an author, illustrator, and character creator represented by Danielle Smith at Red Fox Literary. When not crafting  characters she is shuttling her college-bound athlete to soccer fields, vacuuming up turf-turds, and corralling her seventy-five-pound Doberman lapdog and her fifteen-pound, Brussels-sprout-stealing cat. In her down time, Jenn likes to read, knit, get dragged around the neighborhood by the dog, hurl a kettlebell over her head while whistling the *Bionic Woman* theme song, play Twister on her yoga mat, and ride a horse named Rockets.